BISEXUAL INTERRACIAL EROTICA

JENNIFER'S TOES

JUST PLAIN BOB

WARNING

This book contains sexually explicit scenes and adult language. It may be considered offensive to some readers. This book is for sale to adults ONLY.

Please store your files wisely where they cannot be accessed by underage readers.

* * * * * * * * * * * * * * * * * * *

WANT FREE COPIES OF MY BOOKS?

Just visit my blog and download free copies of my books:

awesomeauthors.org/justplainbob

About the Publisher

4Fun Publishing, a member of **BLVNP Incorporated**, 340 S. Lemon #6200, Walnut CA 91789, info@blvnp.com / legal@blvnp.com
NOTE: Due to the highly emotional reaction of some people to works of erotic fiction, any email sent to the above address that contains foul language or religious references is automatically deleted by our anti-spam software and will not be seen. All other communications are welcome.

DISCLAIMER

Please don't be stupid and kill yourself. This book is a work of FICTION. Do not try any new sexual practice that you find in this book. It is fiction and not to be confused with reality. Neither the author nor the publisher or its associates assume any responsibility for any loss, injury, death or legal consequences resulting from acting on the contents in this book. Every character in this book is over 18 years of age. The author's opinions are not to be construed as the opinions of the publisher. The material in this book is for entertainment purposes ONLY. Enjoy.

Jennifer's Toes

Bisexual Interracial Erotica

By: Just Plain Bob

© Just Plain Bob 2015
ISBN: 978-1-68030-430-5

Chapter 1

As I watched a hard black cock sink into my wife for the seventh or eighth time during the last hour, I wondered just how in the hell my life could have changed so quickly. I glanced over at Jennifer and saw her smiling at me. She beckoned me with her finger said:

"Suck my toes baby; take care of my feet like only you can."

I looked over at Darnell and two of his buddies who were fucking the mindless piece of meat that they had turned my wife Martha into, and then I crawled over to Jennifer and stared licking her feet.

***

It was the toes that started it all. Ten little digits painted blood red and with a design on the big toe of each foot and a toe ring on one toe of the left foot. Jennifer had come to work at our office after transferring in from the home office. I naturally noticed her (as had every other man in the building) because she had a cute face and a nice, trim figure, but I never 'really' noticed her until the office was rearranged and she ended up sitting right across from me. She was there for me to see every time I looked up from what I was doing, and it wasn't long before I was looking up just to be looking at her.

I've always considered myself a well-rounded kind of guy. You hear this guy say he's an ass man, or that guy say he's a leg man or a tit man, but I'm into all of it. Tits, ass, legs, face; I'm not particular at all. If a woman has a good looking face I can admire her all day long even if her body is as thin as a rake handle. I can admire big tits all day even if they come with a face that is as ugly as a mud fence. I just plain love the ladies – period!

Then Jennifer came along and I found out something about myself that I hadn't known. I was a foot lover, or more specifically, I was in love with Jennifer's toes. What I didn't know at the time was that Jennifer knew it. The only time Jennifer's toes were covered was when she wore high heels. Most of the time she wore open toed strappy sandals with a two or three inch heel. Her desk had an open front so her feet were almost always on display and I would be sitting opposite her and admiring the view.

I didn't understand it. I'd seen women's feet in sandals before, and I'd seen them barefoot and with painted toenails, but none of them had ever affected me like Jennifer's. Occasionally I would look up after staring at her feet and catch her looking at me with a bemused smile. A month went by and nothing was said by either of us other than the usual "Good morning" and other pleasantries.

***

The company picnic was when Jen gave me my first raging hard on. Jen showed up with her husband and I, along with everybody else, was surprised to see that he was black. About halfway through the afternoon, I came across Jennifer sitting on a bench and massaging her left foot. She said that she had stepped on something, but couldn't see the sole of her foot:

"Could you please look and see if there is something there?"

I was holding her foot in my hand and was looking at the sole in the area of the instep and I had a sudden desire to kiss it. I was able to fight off the urge, and it was probably a good thing, because her husband came up just then. Jen explained why I had her foot in my hand and he gave me an appraising look, almost as if he knew what was going on in my mind. As the two of them walked off, I wondered if my hard on would be noticeable when I stood up.

***

One day my wife asked me if she could take my Chevy pickup to work so she could move some things. I gave her my keys and took hers and I drove her car to work. Martha's car is a Mustang convertible with the 5.0 liter engine in it and that sucker can fly. I both love and hate to drive it because it gets me in a lot of trouble. I put the top down and get out on the road and the next thing you know I have flashing red and blue lights behind me.

It was a nice day and I drove to work with the top down, and as I pulled into the parking lot at work, Jennifer was just getting out of her Accord. I pulled into a space three down from her and as she came walking my way she said:

"Very nice. When do I get a ride in her?"

"How about lunch time today?"

"You have a date," she said as we walked into the building. *Now why did I do that?* I thought as I made my way to my desk. As I sat down, I wondered if she really meant that she wanted a ride or had she just been making small talk.

Lunchtime came and I was in the middle of something when she walked up to my desk. I looked up at her and she pointed at the clock:

"You do remember offering me a ride, don't you?"

"Yes. Yes, of course. I guess that I let the time get away from me."

She was a picture sitting there in the bucket seat with her hair flying in the breeze as I roared down the highway and I thought, "Oh to be young again." In the restaurant, about halfway through lunch, she said:

"Why have you never asked me to lunch before?"

"I don't know."

"It is plain to me that something about me interests you because I catch you looking at me all the time. So, if I interest you, why haven't you asked me to lunch, or for a drink after work, or maybe even to stop for coffee before work?"

"Well, you and I are both married for one thing, and then there is the difference in our ages. I am almost twice your age."

"Horse feathers! I didn't ask why you haven't tried to take me to bed, just why we never have had lunch or coffee together." Then she smiled and said, "You're afraid of me, aren't you? That's it, the big man is afraid of the little girl."

"No, no, of course not. It just never occurred to me is all. Like I said, we are both married and I was sure that it would have been taken the wrong way. Then of course there is office gossip. I've never taken any of the other women to lunch so you can imagine what my all of a sudden taking you would look like."

"Are you afraid of a bunch of gossipy women?"

"No, I don't guess so."

"Good! I like stirring the pot a little. We will do lunch twice a week from now on. Tuesdays and Fridays will work. Good. That's settled. We really need to make them long lunches to give them something to think about."

It gave me an awful lot to think about too. Why was this beautiful young woman so intent on teasing the girls in the office by making them think that there was something going on between her and a fifty year old man? For the next three weeks Jennifer and I took long lunches on Tuesdays and Fridays, went back to the office, and smiled at each other as we watched the other people in the office cluster around the water cooler or coffee pot, look at us and whisper. It didn't hurt my ego any to have all the younger guys in the office thinking that I was some kind of stud, or to receive the occasional interest glance from some of the other women – but in the back of my mind, there was always a little voice asking what Jennifer was up to.

***

It was a Tuesday and the Chevy truck was halfway to the restaurant, when Jennifer told me to pull over to the side of the road. I did and Jennifer swung her legs up, put her feet on my leg and leaned back against the passenger door:

"I know your secret baby. I've known it since day one and I've waited for you to make a move; but you haven't, so I decided to make it for you. Look at my feet baby. Look at my pretty toes; don't they look sexy? See the nail polish baby? It's fresh. I put it on last night just for you. You love my feet baby and I know it. I watch you watch them every day and I know what you want."

By then I was staring at her feet and I could feel the sweat running down the back of my neck. The sight of her feet and her soothing voice as she crooned, "I know your secret, I know what you want" gave me a hard on.

"I know what you want and I won't let you hide it from me anymore. Suck my toes baby. They are yours right now. Lean over and kiss my feet baby, suck my toes."

I had never in my life done anything like that – I'd never even thought about it – so I surprised myself when I did what she told me to. I leaned down and kissed her feet and she suddenly pulled them away from me and sat up.

"Okay baby, now we know. Find us a motel baby, find us a motel quick."

As I pulled away from the side of the road, she slid over next to me and reached down and squeezed my cock with her hand:

"Don't lose this baby, don't lose this."

It was some heady shit: a beautiful twenty-six year old woman telling a fifty year old man to hurry up and get her to a motel. I unzipped myself and let my cock out of confinement and Jennifer giggled "Oh you randy old man you" as she took hold of it and stroked it. It was a five-minute ride to the Best Western and it was with great reluctance that I took my cock away from Jennifer's hands to go inside and get a room. Once in the room Jennifer hurried straight to the bed and sat down on it. No kissing or anything like that, just "Hurry baby, we don't have much time."

I started to loosen my tie and she said, "No baby, just trousers and briefs. Hurry baby, hurry."

When my pants were off, I walked to the bed and she stood up, pushed me down on my back and then she lay down next to me, but with her feet toward my head. I thought she was getting ready for a sixty-nine and I reached for her hips.

"No, not that baby, my feet. Do my feet baby, lick my feet, suck my toes."

She had latched onto my cock and she was stroking it as she crooned:

"Kiss them baby, lick them, suck my toes baby, make love to my feet baby and I'll get you off. I'll make you cum baby, I'll get you off."

I was looking at her feet as she was stroking my cock and for some reason, even though I'd never done it before, loving Jennifer's feet seemed to be the most natural thing in the world for me to do. I kissed and licked and sucked on her toes and I quickly discovered that one of Jennifer's erogenous zones was the instep of her foot. When I would lick the arch of her foot, her body would shudder and I began to wonder if Jennifer could orgasm from nothing more than attention to her feet. I was working hard to find out and at the same time her hand job had me close to coming. I kept waiting for her to take me into her mouth or turn and tell me to fuck her, but she kept working my dick with her hands and then I found out that hands is all it was going to be:

"Cum for me baby, I want your cum on my fingers. Come on baby, shoot for me, let me see it shoot out," and then she shoved a finger in my ass and I blew like Old Faithful.

"Oh wow baby, I'm glad you weren't in my mouth. That one would have blown a hole in the back of my throat."

Saying "Don't move," she got off the bed and came back moments later with a wash cloth and cleaned up my cock and stomach and then it was, "Come on baby, we need to get back to work" and she tossed me my pants.

***

The first half of the ride back to work was quiet as I sat behind the wheel wondering just what the hell had happened. Checking into a motel with a beautiful girl led me to expect a little more than what I got. Jennifer interrupted my thoughts:

"Confused?

"I'd have to say a big yes to that."

"It is simple baby, my feet are very sensitive and I love to have them kissed and licked. There aren't many men around who are into feet and who will do for me what you did. I've watched you watch my feet for a couple of months now and I thought that you might just be my kind of man, so today I decided to find out one way or the other. Happily, you are, but all I could do for you today was a hand job. The reason for that is that I have to have my husband's permission before I can let you make love to me."

"Your husband gives you permission to go to bed with other men?"

She shrugged, "What can I say? We are both a little on the kinky side. Anyway, I wasn't sure about you so I haven't asked him yet if I could make love with you or at least suck your cock. If he lets me, are you willing to be my foot slave?"

How do you answer something like that? I couldn't deny that I was attracted to her and her sexy feet and what fifty year old man wouldn't give his left nut to fuck a sexy twenty-six year old young woman? But I was over my head there. A husband who gives his wife permission to fuck other men? A wife who asks for it? And just what in the hell was a foot slave? Once again Jennifer interrupted my thoughts:

"While you are thinking about it baby, think ahead to this Friday. Have you ever had a foot job? I can't fuck you without Darrell's okay, and I won't ask for his okay until you agree to be my foot slave, but I can still make you feel good. Think of it baby, think of my ten pretty toes rubbing your cock and making you shoot your juice all over the place."

We pulled into the parking lot at work and she slid over next to me, put her hand on my cock and squeezed it gently as she kissed me. Her tongue darted into my mouth and then she pulled away:

"You have the name baby, wouldn't you like to play the game?"

"What?"

She nodded toward the window and I saw that several co-workers returning from lunch had seen the kiss.

***

That Tuesday changed me more than I cared to admit. Until then Jennifer and I had been playing a harmless game. Suddenly it wasn't a game anymore and I was presented with two very conflicting emotions. The first was obvious – I wanted Jennifer! I wanted her so bad, I was seriously considering saying yes to being her foot slave without knowing what that really meant. The other was just as obvious, at least to me. I felt an overwhelming sense of guilt. For the very first time, I had been unfaithful to my wife of twenty-seven years and I was already thinking of doing it again. Hell, I wasn't just thinking of doing it again, I was already looking forward to it.

I loved Martha and we had a good marriage, but what man my age in his right mind would take a pass on Jennifer? Martha was in great shape for a woman of forty-eight and she still turned heads whenever she went somewhere. She was fun loving and our sex life was still three and sometimes four times a week. I had no complaints and no real reason to stray, but she was still a grandmother and she looked it and acted it. Jennifer was young, vibrant, and sexy as hell. Looking back on it, I guess it was a case of me looking back and seeing that my youth had disappeared, and then looking forward and seeing nothing but old age waiting for me. Jennifer could make me young again.

***

The time between Tuesday and Friday dragged. Every day I would sit and look over at Jennifer and when she saw me looking, she would wiggle her toes and smile at me. Luckily, Martha and I had made love Thursday night or Friday morning. I would have had to go to the men's room and masturbate to keep from coming too quick when Jennifer and I got to the motel. On the ride to the motel, Jennifer turned to me:

"How good are you at taking tests baby?"

"What do you mean?"

"I asked Darnell for permission and he said that he didn't think an older man like you would be kinky enough, so he gave me a little test for you. If you pass it, you get to fuck my brains out. If not, well, we've had some fun, right?"

"What's the test?"

"Wait until we get to the room baby, I don't want to scare you off too early."

Once in the room, Jennifer quickly stripped and stood before me smiling as I undressed. She was absolute perfection and again I asked myself, "Why me?" She could have had her pick of any of the good looking younger men in the office, so why me? When I was naked Jennifer got on the bed and said, "You know what I want lover." I lowered my head to her feet and she said, "Turn lover, turn so I can get my hands on your cock." I repositioned myself and her warm hands went to work on my cock as I began making love to her feet.

For several minutes we worked on each other, and then Jennifer asked me to tell her when I was close. I told her that I was there and she pulled away from me and told me to get on my back and that she was going to finish me with her feet. I did what she said and she took my cock between both of her feet, pressed them together and started working them up and down.

"Cum for me baby, cum for me. Show my feet that you really love them. Come on lover, cum for me."

It was too much. I watched those blood red painted toes moving up and down my cock and I erupted. The sperm bubbled out of my cock and then ran down it and all over Jennifer's toes.

"Are you ready to take your test baby? Are you ready to show me how kinky you can be?"

"What? What do you want me to do?"

"Lick my feet lover. Clean your cum off my feet. Lick up every last little bit baby. Clean between my toes and don't leave a speck behind and then this sexy body can be yours lover."

I scrambled around so that I could get busy on her feet. Not much of a test, as far as I was concerned. One of Martha's favorite things was my eating her pussy after I had cum in it, so I was no stranger to the taste of my own cum. As I licked and lapped, I thought of the prize that waited – Jennifer's hot, sexy body – and my cock started to grow again. I finished my task and then I looked up at her:

"Did I pass?"

"Oh yes baby, did you ever."

I moved up to claim my reward and she scooted away. "We can't baby, not just yet. I have to tell Darnell first. He said you had to pass the test, and you did lover, you did. But I still have to let him know first. Next time baby, next time I'll be all yours."

She saw my hard cock, "Poor baby. I can't let you take that back to the office. Whatever would they think of me if they saw that tent in your trousers?"

She gave me a hand job, then we dressed and headed back to work. It was a quiet ride and we were pulling into the lot at work when she said:

"I'm sorry baby. I guess that I should have made it clear that nothing would happen today, but I was in such a hurry to get Darnell's test out of the way that I just didn't think. I want you baby. I want you so badly that it hurts, and I'm so anxious to have you that I'm not thinking clearly."

She slid over next to me, took my head in her hands and kissed me. Her tongue slipped into my mouth and things got a little steamy as I sent my tongue into her mouth. Jennifer broke the kiss and said, "Damn, that wasn't very smart of me."

"What?"

"Kissing you like that with everybody watching. One of those women is going to wonder what it is that you have, and she will try and move in on my baby."

I looked and saw a good half dozen of my co-workers looking our way as they returned from lunch.

"Next time baby. Once I tell Darnell you passed the test, we will be clear to go. Can you wait for that for me baby? Can you wait three more days?"

***

I didn't have any choice but to wait. The afternoon went by quickly, but then time started to drag. The weekend seemed to take forever to go by. At one point Martha asked me what was the matter.

"You seem so preoccupied honey, is something wrong?"

"No sweetie, just something at work that didn't get taken care of and I'm hoping that I can get it done when I go back in on Monday."

Martha and I made love that night, and when it was over and she was softly snoring beside me, I laid there looking up at the ceiling and wondering just what the fuck was wrong with me. I had a loving wife who had been sexually satisfying me for twenty-eight years, so why was I risking it for a twenty-six year old unknown? Jennifer had a young, firm, well-toned body, but that didn't mean she was a good lay. Martha was not young, firm and well-toned; but she gave superb head, loved anal and was multi-orgasmic when I made love to her. I loved her and I didn't want to spend my life with anyone else but her, so what the hell was I doing? I saw Jennifer in my mind and I saw her wiggling her toes and my cock twitched. Shit! I rolled over on my side and tried to go to sleep.

***

Jennifer was sitting in her car when I pulled into the company lot on Monday. Before I had even turned off my ignition she got out of her car and hurried over to mine, got in and slid over next to me:

"Kiss me lover; give the office gossips something to work with."

While we swapped tongues, her hand pulled down my zipper and she reached inside to fondle my cock.

"Did you think about me all weekend baby? All I thought about every hour was what we are going to do tomorrow baby. Darnell told me that I could, lover; I've got the go ahead. You still want me baby? My toes missed you lover. Now that we have Darnell's permission, maybe you can get out of the house next Saturday or Sunday so we can spend some quality time together. Would you like that lover? Oh shit baby, put that away before I'm tempted to give you a blow job right here in the parking lot. We're going to be late baby, tuck it away," and she slid out of the car and walked away leaving me with a case of blue balls.

All day I looked over at Jennifer and saw her smiling at me and she would glance down, and when I followed her glance, I would end up looking at her toes and my cock would twitch. I had it bad – I had it real bad. About ten, Jennifer asked me to give her a hand getting something out of the supply room. We were no sooner in the door than she turned and kissed me. She ran her hand down my front until she got to my cock and began to squeeze it. She broke the kiss:

"God baby, I want you so bad. I don't want to wait until tomorrow, but I promised my sister I'd have lunch with her today."

She kissed me again, and just as I slipped my tongue into her mouth, the door opened and Maude from Accounting came in and saw us. "Oh excuse me," she said and she turned and left.

Jennifer giggled and said, "I was about two seconds from going to my knees and taking you in my mouth. The next twenty-four hours are going to drive me crazy, baby. I don't want to wait." She kissed me again and said, "We'd best get back to work before I pull you down and make you take me right here on the floor."

I didn't get a damned thing done that day. All I did was look at Jennifer and think about the next day.

***

I didn't get anything done the next morning either. I'd look at Jennifer and then at the clock and tried to will the time to pass quickly. Naturally, just the opposite happened. Seconds seemed like minutes and minutes seemed like hours. Finally lunchtime arrived and I was so keyed up that I pushed Jennifer away when she slid over next to me in the truck.

"If you touch me, I'll cum in my pants. You have me so hot right now that it is all I can do to keep from pulling over to the side of the road and doing you right here in the daylight in front of God and everybody."

"I turn you on, baby?"

"Oh God yes."

"I have a surprise for you baby. I'm so eager for this that I stopped and got the room on the way to work this morning so you wouldn't have to waste time checking in. Park outside room 121 baby."

I entered room 121 to find a naked black man who I recognized as Jennifer's husband sitting on the bed. I turned to Jennifer and saw her taking off her clothes. She turned her head away and said:

"Sorry baby, but he didn't believe me when I told him that you passed his little test. He thinks I'm so hot for you that I lied. He doesn't believe that a white man your age would do such a thing and he wants to see for himself. Be patient with me baby, I'll make it up to you, I promise."

Darnell ignored me and watched his wife. "Hurry up damn it, I got things to do."

Once naked Jennifer got on the bed and spread her legs, "Hurry up Darnell. I want him and you're wasting our lunch hour."

Darnell got between her legs and started fucking her while I stood there and watched. I was torn between running from the room and staying to watch. I saw Jennifer on the bed, sex personified, and my cock grew hard. She moaned, she groaned, she clutched and grabbed and all I could think was, "Hurry the fuck up Darnell so I can be the one she clutches and grabs."

Then Darnell grunted, "You ready baby?" and Jennifer said, "Yes, let's just get it over with."

Darnell pulled out of his wife and Jennifer swung around and put her feet, those oh so sexy feet, on the floor. Darnell grabbed his cock, stroked it a couple of times and then he came all over her toes.

"There it is white boy, clean it up."

I stood there dumbfounded and was on the verge of bolting from the room when Jennifer cried, "Do it baby, please do it. Hurry baby, I want you and we only have an hour for lunch. Please baby, please."

I forced myself to believe that it was just the mental idea that I found repulsive – sucking up another man's cum – and that the taste wouldn't be all that different from mine. And then there was Jennifer, legs spread, finger fucking herself and begging me to hurry. I knelt down and started cleaning her feet.

"Oh yes baby, oh God yes. Please hurry baby, I want you so bad."

I was almost done when Darnell said, "That's only the first half of the test white boy; to pass, you have to clean this off too," and he pushed his cock at me.

"Hurry baby, hurry, do what he wants. I'm going crazy here baby, I need your cock in me, hurry baby, hurry."

My only excuse was that I was inflamed with passion. Jennifer was begging me to hurry and I wanted her so bad, and time was running out so I stuck my tongue out and licked the head of Darnell's cock.

Jennifer cried out, "No baby, no. Licking will take too long and we are running out of time. Just take it in your mouth baby; one quick suck and it will be clean and you can come to me."

Again, all I can say is that I was out of my mind with lust for Jennifer and all I could think about was getting on the bed with her, and so I opened my mouth, took Darnell's cock in and I sucked on it. His hands went to the back of my head and he held me on him and said, "Clean it good whitey, get it all."

"Hurry baby, for God's sake hurry. I'm so hot baby, please hurry, just get it over with so we can be together."

Just get it over with, I said to myself, just get it over with so you can get to Jennifer. I sucked on Darnell and I licked and suddenly I felt him start to grow. I panicked and tried to pull back, but he was holding onto my head with both hands. I put my hands on the floor and braced myself to push up and away from him, but before I could do it Jennifer slid off the bed, got behind me and wrapped her arms around me. She held me tight while crooning in my ear:

"That was very good white boy, that was excellent. You and I are going to have a lot of fun together," and then he surprised the hell out of me. He grabbed my head in both hands and he kissed me. He pushed his tongue in my mouth, swirled it around and then broke the kiss. "Oh yes whitey, we are going to have a lot of fun together."

Jennifer was still stroking my cock and she was crooning, "Cum for me baby, cum for me" and I shot all over the floor." She stood up and said, "Now that wasn't so bad, was it? It looked to me like you liked it." Turning to Darnell she asked, "Did you get it?"

"Oh yeah baby, all of it, I got it all."

"Good," she said and she picked up her clothes and started dressing. She saw me looking at her and she said, "Sorry baby, but Darnell doesn't let anyone but his friends fuck me and all of his friends are black." She saw the confusion on my face, "You got off baby. I saw to it that you got your rocks off. I might be a bitch, but I wouldn't leave anyone who sucks my toes like you do hanging. Come on baby, hurry up and dress or we will be late getting back from lunch."

***

On the ride back to work Jennifer wouldn't look at me; she kept her head turned so she could look out the side window. Finally I couldn't take it any more:

"What the hell is this all about Jennifer?"

She looked at me and shrugged, "I guess there is no sense in not telling you since Darnell will be talking to you about it tomorrow or the next day anyway. Darnell wants something from you that you wouldn't normally let him have, so he had to do something to make sure of you."

"What could he possibly want from me?"

"He wants your wife."

"What? Are you out of your mind?"

"Afraid not, baby. He met her at the company picnic and she fired him up and he decided that he is going to fuck her."

"What do you mean by she 'fired him up'?"

"She's of a type that black men like, baby. Nice big shapely butt, big pillow like tits and she's damned sexy looking for an older broad."

"Tell Darnell to go to hell. It just ain't going to happen."

"Of course it is baby and you are going to help."

"The hell I will."

"Of course you will baby. You were so hot to get my body that you didn't pay a whole lot of attention to much else, like the video camera on the shelf with the towels. Darnell has you on tape baby. He had video of you licking his cum off of my toes and then sucking his cock. He thinks that there is a lot you might be willing to do to keep that tape from going public."

I stared at her in horror as what she was saying hit home.

Chapter 2

"My God, that would ruin me," I cried when Jennifer told me of the videotape.

"I think that's the idea baby. If you don't want to be ruined then you do what Darnell wants. Shouldn't be all that hard baby, all he wants is to fuck your wife."

I pulled into the parking lot at work and then sat there staring out the window. "All this, all this toe sucking, all this "Are you kinky enough" was just bullshit? You set out to sucker me all along?"

"Well, yes and no. It isn't all bullshit. Yes I did set out to hook you, but as for the toe and foot business, I really do get off when a man loves my feet. I wasn't totally one way about it baby. I did get you off every time with hand jobs and foot jobs and I'll keep on getting you off that way. If Darnell gets what he wants he may even let me give you a blow job or two."

"But only if I let him fuck my wife."

"You aren't letting him do anything baby. He will fuck your wife with or without your help."

"I doubt that very much. Martha just isn't that kind of woman."

"Oh? What do you want to bet that Martha isn't sitting at home right now thinking that you aren't that kind of man? But you are aren't you?"

"What is it that you want from me?"

"To short-cut the process."

"I don't understand."

"It is simple enough baby. The regular process would be to study her habits, find out where she goes and when and then arrange to meet her. Once that was done the only worry left would be a husband getting in the way. The tape gets you out of the way and gives Darnell a way to bypass the process. You will invite us over for dinner some night and Darnell will take it from there and all you have to do then is stay out of the way."

"That's it? Darnell will take it from there?"

"Honey, Darnell has the same gift that I have. I've known since I was twelve years old that there were some men I could wrap around my little finger and you are one of them baby. Darnell knew that he could have your wife the minute he met her. It is a done deal baby, get used to it. Now get over here and kiss me baby so we can give our adoring public something to gossip about."

"I don't think so, Jennifer. I don't much like you anymore."

"Hey lover," she said with a touch of steel in her voice, "You do what I want, when I want or you will end up being very, very sorry."

"What are you going to do, show the tape? I don't think so. You do that and you have no more leverage over me. Darnell might not like that."

"I don't need to show the tape baby. I just have to plant ideas in Darnell's head. He was serious when he said he liked the way you sucked him off. Want to have to do it some more, maybe a lot more? I can arrange it for you. Now get over here and kiss me and you had damned well better make it look good."

I hesitated a moment, but I realized that my hand wasn't all that strong and that I might as well throw my cards in. I did what she said and the kiss was as steamy as she could make it, and when we broke I asked her:

"Now that you've done the damage and got what you were after, why the kiss?"

"Because I like you baby and you and I are still going to have fun. Granted, it will only be hand jobs and foot jobs, but how many men your age are even getting that much from a twenty-six year old? I love my husband baby and I do what he wants. Doesn't mean I'm necessarily happy doing some of what I do, but for him I do it. I have hopes for you and me. If Darnell gets what he wants, he's happy; and when he's happy he lets me do things that I want. I don't know if he will ever let me fuck you, but I'm pretty sure that he will let me give you head. I'd like to be able to do that for you baby, I really would." She patted my leg, "Come on lover, let's not be late."

***

I was trapped. I had no way out. I couldn't confess to Martha because I knew her well enough to know she would pack up and be gone. That Darnell would have his way with her was just too ridiculous to even think about, but I had no choice when it came to doing what Darnell wanted. Just a video capture of me with his cock in my mouth would destroy me, both socially and financially. If it got out, I'd not only lose my customer base, which would kill my commissions, but the divorce would end up taking everything that I had.

I was so preoccupied with my predicament that I hadn't even looked over at Jennifer. I'd totally forgotten about her so it was surprise when she walked up to my desk and tapped my shoulder to get my attention:

"I got the motel room for the day, sugar, and Darnell wants to talk with you, so meet me there after work."

The door to the room was open when I got there and I walked in to find Jennifer sitting on the bed. "Close the door baby. Darnell won't be here until six and that gives us some time alone." She kicked off her sandals, "Come on over here baby; suck my toes while I give you a hand job."

I just stood there and stared at her.

"Come on baby, you know that you want to. I know that you're pissed at me, but you still want to suck my toes, you know you do. Come on baby, I'll make you feel good."

I did it. God only knows why, but I did it. I licked her feet and sucked on her toes and she gave me a hand job while I did it. We were cleaned up and dressed when Darnell arrived. He got right to the point:

"She tell you the deal?"

"Yes."

"The way it will go is that you will invite us over for a barbecue on Saturday. You will drink too much and go and lay down. That's not a lot to ask in exchange for the tape, now is it?"

"That's it?"

"That's it. You do that and I give you the tape."

"Even if she laughs in your face?"

"She won't do that. I saw it in her eyes at your company picnic. By Sunday morning you will be a cuckolded husband, I guarantee it."

He saw the look on my face and said, "I know you don't believe it, but she can be had and I'd be willing to bet that I won't be her first."

"No way! Martha just isn't that kind of woman."

He looked at me contemplatively, "You really love her?"

"Yes I do."

"Enough to save her from a fate worse than death – namely me?"

I didn't even have to think about that one. "Yes."

"Okay. Here is a one-time offer. I liked the feel of your mouth on my joint today. Be my bitch for a week and I'll give you the tape, but I want an answer right now. Come over here, suck my cock and then do it whenever I want for a week and you get the tape. Do a really nice job and I'll let Jennifer suck your dick, but it has to be right now. You have thirty seconds."

Looking back on it, it was the most disastrous decision I ever made, but at the time it seemed like a no brainer. I'd already sucked his cock once. Granted that it was more of a mouth rape than a consensual blow job, but I had sucked him off and it hadn't killed me. So if I did it a couple of more times I'd get the tape back and keep him away from Martha; and if I did good I'd get head from Jennifer. A no brainer.

"Okay, I'll do it."

"Good man. I was hoping that you would say that. Nothing turns this nigger on more than having a white man on his knees."

He took off his clothes and sat down on the side of the bed and crooked a finger at me, "Come on bitch, get over here and suck my joint."

I walked over and went to my knees in front of him and proceeded to give him the best blow job I was capable of giving. I was determined to make it good enough that I would get at least a blow job from Jennifer for all the hell I'd been through. I licked and sucked and I kept working more and more of his cock into my mouth, trying my best to deep throat him. I did everything that I loved having Martha do to me and I made Darnell moan with pleasure.

I felt hands tugging on my belt and I looked down to see Jennifer take my cock out and stroke it. She jacked me off for a minute or so and then she lay down and her feet took the place of her hands. I felt her toes rub my balls and my whole body tingled. I started playing with Darnell's balls and he moaned again:

"God Damn white boy, but you are a fucking natural at this. I'm going to love you being my bitch. I should have asked for a month instead of a week. That's it bitch, suck it, make me cum bitch, make me fire right down your throat."

I felt his cock throb and then he was letting loose in my mouth, and I swallowed his stuff as fast as it poured out of the end of his cock. I got the last drop and then I licked his cock clean.

"Keep it in your mouth bitch. Get it hard and I'll make your day." I kept sucking on him and said, "Get naked Jenn. We are going to give my bitch a treat."

Jennifer stripped down, got on the bed and started fingering herself while I worked on getting Darnell up again. It took me all of two minutes and then he pulled out of my mouth, got on the bed and started fucking Jennifer. He turned to look at me and said, "Get ready bitch, just watch and get ready."

Get ready for what? I wondered as I remained on my knees with my cock throbbing. I was hurting. Jennifer had me almost to the point of cumming when Darnell had had her stop and get naked, and watching him fuck her was only making it worse. I reached down to stroke my cock and Darnell barked:

"Leave your cock alone bitch. I'll tell you when you can get off."

A few minutes later he said, "Here it comes" and Jennifer cried, "Hurry baby, hurry, I'm cumminggggggggg....." and she had her orgasm. Darnell pulled his soft cock out of her and I saw a touch of cum leak from her cunt lips.

"There's your gift from me bitch. Clean out her pussy. Get in a sixty-nine with him Jenn and suck the white boy off."

Why in God's name Darnell wanted me sucking him off when he had Jennifer, I'll never understand. I had always considered Martha's blow jobs as state of the art, but Jennifer made Martha seem like a teenaged beginner. Her mouth was magic and she made me forget all the bad things that had happened that day. I was on the bottom and she was on top as I feasted on her pussy and she sucked my cock, and I thought that must be what Heaven was supposed to be like. She was humping her pussy down at my mouth as she was making the same noises she made when she had orgasmed while being fucked by Darnell. I was sucking on her clit when she pulled her head of my cock and cried out:

"Oh sweet mother fucking Jesus. He made me cum with his mouth Darnell; he made me cum with his mouth. Oh god, oh sweet fucking god." Her body shook and then she lowered her head and captured the head of my cock as I erupted.

"Damn white boy, you two really know how to put on a show," Darnell said. "Look at what you did to me," and he pointed at his rock hard cock. "Get over here bitch and take care of it."

***

For the next five days Jennifer and I would hit the motel at lunch and I would suck her toes while she sucked my cock. At night on the way home from work, I would stop at their house and give Darnell his blow job while Jennifer worked on mine. Darnell once said he was sorry that he'd only asked for a week instead of a month and I was sorry he hadn't also. Not that I was having all that much fun sucking his cock, but I was going to miss Jennifer's mouth.

The seventh day, as I was ready to go to lunch, I stopped by Jennifer's desk, "Ready to go sweetie?"

"Not today baby. I've got things on my mind and I don't feel much like it."

"Maybe tonight when I stop by?"

"Yeah baby, maybe tonight."

I was disappointed that we didn't do lunch because it would have been our last time. That night was the night I was to complete my bargain with Darnell and get the damning tape back, and I knew that was going to end my weird relationship with Jennifer.

Jennifer met me at the door and gave me a sad smile as she said, "He's waiting for you in the bedroom."

"You aren't joining us?"

"Not tonight baby. Better hurry, he's anxious."

I entered the room and Darnell was already naked and on the bed. "Hurry up bitch, I need release like only you can give me."

I took off my suit coat and tie and knelt down beside the bed and he said, "No baby, get naked."

I stripped and got on the bed and sucked him off. He came and I swallowed it all and then licked his cock clean and he said, "Crawl up here baby," and he took my arms and pulled me up until I was laying on top of him and then he kissed me. His tongue probed my mouth and I felt my cock rubbing against his limp dick and it felt so weird. He broke the kiss and said:

"Kiss me back baby, just this one time kiss me back," and he kissed me again. *What the fuck*, I thought, I've sucked his cock for a week now. A little tongue won't hurt and this is the last time I'll see him, so I kissed him the way I kissed his wife and mine. It was a long kiss and just a little steamy and I felt his cock twitch. He broke the kiss and said:

"I told you that you were going to be my bitch and for a week now you have been great. I don't want to lose you baby, so I'm going to make you my bitch permanently."

His arms tightened around me and he said, "Don't fight it baby, just go with the flow and it will be over quickly. You'll love it baby. Anyone who sucks cock as well as you do is bound to love it."

I hadn't heard them come into the room. There were four of them and as soon as they had me held down, Darnell let go of me and had them get me up on my knees. I felt the cold wetness on Darnell's fingers as he began to work them in me. Suddenly I knew what he was going to do and I struggled and tried to break free of the hands holding me, but I had no chance against the four men who had pinned me down. I screamed at them, I threatened them and I swore I would kill every fucking one of them when I got loose, and all the while Darnell was crooning in my ear:

"Relax baby, relax and it will only hurt for a minute. Relax and go with the flow baby. It is going to happen so you might as well relax and let it happen. Who knows, you might even like it."

When he felt he had me loose enough, he moved behind me and I felt the burning pain as he worked his cock into my ass. I screamed out and tears ran down my face and I hurt, oh god did I hurt. Darnell kept fucking me slow and easy, and after several minutes, it didn't hurt so bad, but I was still sobbing into a pillow when I suffered the final indignity. My cock had gotten hard and without even being touched it shot all over the bed sheet in under me and one of the men laughed and said, "God damn, he likes it, he really likes it."

After that it was a blur as the five men took turns fucking me and shoving their cocks into my mouth. Then it was over and only Darnell and I were left in the room.

"Now you are really my bitch."

"Why? Why did you do this to me? What did I ever do to you to make you want to do this to me?"

"You sucked my cock baby. You sucked it better than anyone except Jenn and when I find a great cock sucker I hang on to them. You are my complete bitch now baby, and I'm not letting you go."

I got up off the bed and said as I started to get dressed, "Oh no, tonight is the end. I gave you your week and now give me the tape so I can get out of here."

"Tapes on the dresser."

I went over and picked it up, looked at it for a second and then dropped it in my suit coat pocket. It made me feel like the weight of the world had been lifted off of me.

"Just so you know, I made a copy of it."

I turned to face him, anger on my face, and he said, "It is just for me baby. A deal is a deal and I promise you that no one else will ever see it."

For some reason I believed him and I turned to go. I had just reached the door when Darnell said, "Oh, by the way, is next Saturday good for you?"

"Good for what?"

"To have me and Jenn over so I can take my shot at your wife."

I laughed at him. I patted my pocket where the tape was, "Sorry, but you don't have the leverage anymore."

"Baby, you have got to be the dumbest white man ever to be born. No, I don't have that tape any more, but I do have the one I made the night I made you the deal for that one and I have the ones I made every night you stopped here. I also have the one from our little fun fest tonight. You are my bitch baby, until I get tired of you. Who knows, your wife might be so good that she can be my permanent bitch and I'll leave you alone. Now go on home and set up my meeting with your wife."

***

I stumbled from the room, despair filling every atom of my body, and headed for the front door. Jennifer was sitting on the couch and she got up and followed me to the door and then she put a hand on my arm.

"I'm sorry baby, it was never my intent to see you suffer any physical pain."

I slapped her hand away from me, "Save your fucking phony ass sympathy, Jennifer. You've fucking destroyed me and now you are going to get together with that asshole you are married to and try and destroy my marriage. You are a treacherous snake Jennifer and I'd just as soon never set eyes on you again."

I spit in her face and I walked out the door.

Chapter 3

Martha wanted to make love when I got home that night, and as she gave me a blow job, I looked down at her bobbing head and realized just how much I did love her. I couldn't – no, I wouldn't – expose her to Darnell and Jennifer. After what had been done to me earlier that evening, I knew that things would just get worse for me and that eventually it would get out that I had been sucking cock and had been gangbanged in my ass.

I was damned if I did and damned if I didn't and I was not going to drag Martha down with me. I would probably lose her when she received a copy of whichever tape Darnell decided to send her, but at least she wouldn't be exposed to whatever perversion that Darnell and Jennifer had planned for her.

After an extremely satisfying session of love making, I fell asleep holding Martha in my arms and had the first really good night's sleep since the whole thing with Jennifer had started.

***

The next morning Jennifer was sitting in her car waiting when I pulled onto the company lot. She got out of her car and headed for mine intending to get in on the passenger side. I hit the automatic door lock just as she was reaching for the handle and then quickly got out on my side and headed for the building. Once inside I went straight to my desk, sat down and turned on my computer. I pulled up the word processing program and began my letter of resignation. Jennifer had come up behind me and was reading over my shoulder.

"That's a dumb thing to do baby."

"I didn't ask for your input. In fact, as I remember it, I told you that I never wanted to lay eyes on you again."

"I know baby, but I also know that you didn't mean it. You were angry at what happened and I just happened to be convenient for you to lash out at."

"Jennifer, you set me up and you did it deliberately. The whole purpose behind what you did was to be able to ruin me if I didn't give in to your fucking blackmail. Everything that has happened to me has happened because of you. You have managed to see to it that I don't even like myself anymore, that I'm disgusted with myself. Oh yes I did mean it when I said I'd just as soon never see you again."

"Let me tell you something mister! I didn't force you to do a damned thing. You did everything on your own right up to and including licking Darnell's cock. You were not forced to lick him off my feet and you crawled to him and took his cock in your mouth. Okay, so the first full blow job wasn't completely voluntary, but you did every one after that willingly and furthermore, you liked it! You can deny it all you want baby, but nobody who sees you suck a cock will ever doubt for one minute that you like doing it and you are so good doing it that anyone who sees you do it is going to want one too.

"You have it in your head that somehow you are less of a man because you suck cock, but that's all bullshit. All it is, is that you now have another facet of your sexual being to enjoy. As for last night, okay, I'll give you that it was a shock to your system, but you liked it sweetie. I've watched the tape and it shines through – you liked it! As far as this 'less of a man' shit is concerned, you have only to ask yourself if you enjoy sex with your wife any less lately than before and you will have your answer.

"Be pissed at me all you want sweetie, but I did give you a fuller sex life and you fucking well know it!"

She turned on her heel and went to her desk and I turned back to my letter of resignation. I finished it and put it in my center desk drawer and then got busy on the stuff in my basket.

***

Ten minutes before lunch I walked over to my desk and sat down. I had made a determined effort not to look Jennifer's way all morning so I assumed that she had gotten the message that I really did not want to have anything more to do with her. I was surprised when she came over to my desk and said:

"Are we still on for lunch?"

"Get away from me Jennifer."

"Oh come on sweetie, surely you aren't so mad at me that you will pass up a perfectly good blow job. You won't have to do anything at all for it, I promise."

I turned my back on her and she said, "Come on baby, don't be that way. I'm the same girl that you've lusted after for the last two weeks and Darnell is so happy with you that I have blanket permission to give you head whenever you want it. Come on baby, let me show you that I really do like you."

I turned and looked at her, but before I could say a word she said, "I'm perfectly capable of making a scene sweetie, so why be uncomfortable here in the office with people staring at you when you could be having a good time with me."

It was obvious that she wasn't going to leave me alone and I did have a certain curiosity as to what trick she planned to play on me this time. Well, if she did, I had one to play on her. I wouldn't hesitate to drive away and leave her standing at the motel. What could she do, ruin me? That was going to happen anyway when I submitted my letter of resignation and confessed to Martha.

She surprised me when we got to the motel. "Just take off your trousers baby, today is all about you."

She gave me one of her world class blow jobs and swallowed everything my cock spit out and then she asked me if I would like her to make me hard and do it again. Naturally, I said yes and she did it. As we were driving back to work she said:

"Darnell wanted me to ask you what time we should be over on Saturday."

"Tell him I've decided that I'm not going to do it."

"That isn't a really smart move, baby."

"I've decided to just go ahead and let you ruin me rather than subject Martha to your sick games. After what the two of you did to me, I can only guess at what kind of sick shit you might pull on Martha."

"You love her that much? You would actually let Darnell follow through on his threat just to protect your wife?"

"Yes I would."

"That's so sweet baby, but then you would never know, would you?

"Know what?"

"Whether she was worthy of your sacrifice. You would never know whether she turned Darnell down or not. You would always wonder about it from now on. I told you that Darnell has a way with a certain kind of woman, just like I have a way with men like you. Darnell says he saw it in her eyes and he knows he can get her. You will always wonder if she would have given in or not. Why not find out? If she doesn't, you can laugh at Darnell, and boy does he hate to be laughed at.

If she does, well, that just means she is a slightly flawed person, much like yourself.

"And think about this sweetie, he is still going to go after her. All this stuff with the tapes was just to make it easier for him to get close to her. Right now you are in the loop and know everything that is going on. You bail out now, and two weeks or two months from now, when Darnell makes his move, you won't know about it. Think about it baby. Wouldn't you like to know for sure?"

I didn't know how to answer that. I didn't know it at the time, but she had planted a question that was going to nag at me for days. When we got back to work she said:

"Can you stop by tonight? Darnell got so turned on by the way we sixty-nined the other night that he wants us to do it again. Please baby, for me?"

***

You would have thought that I would have known better by then, but I did stop by their place on the way home. Jennifer gave me a big smile when she opened the door. "Oh goodie, I was hoping you would show."

She took my hand and pulled me into the living room where Darnell was watching TV with two other black guys. "Darnell honey, look who's here."

Darnell looked over at me and smiled, "Hi baby, how's my favorite bitch?"

Before I could reply, he turned to the other two men and said, "Hey, you guys want to see a really hot show?"

They both said yes and he said, "The bedroom will be more comfortable, let's go." He and the two men got up and headed for the room, and Jennifer took my hand and pulled me along after her. In the bedroom Darnell said, "Okay baby, do your thing," and Jennifer stripped and got on the bed and started fingering her pussy. The two men stripped and joined her on the bed, one getting between her legs and one moving up near her head so he could shove his cock in her mouth. She pushed her cunt up at the man between her legs and greedily went after the cock in her mouth. Darnell turned to me and said:

"See why I love the bitch? She is an absolute slut. I hope that you will be the same way for me."

He took my hand and carried it down in front of him and I felt that he had taken his cock out. He put my hand on it and said, "Look at her. Have you ever seen anything so wanton in your life?" On the bed, Jennifer was going crazy trying to push herself up on the cock in her pussy and deep throat the man in her mouth, and my dick got hard as a rock. Darnell's hand was moving mine on his cock as we watched Jennifer and the two men. I wasn't aware when his hand fell away, but suddenly I noticed that I was stroking his cock all by myself. He turned to me, kissed me and said:

"Please? Because you want to and not because you are being forced or tricked? Come on baby, I need it and I want you."

As I went to my knees in front of him, I thought back to what Jennifer had said earlier, "You liked it. You can deny it all you want, but you liked it."

On the bed, the man in Jennifer's cunt announced that he was coming and when he had, he changed places with the one getting the blow job. By the time the second man had cum in Jennifer, Darnell had cum down my throat and had me on my knees pushing his cock in my ass. Jennifer beamed at me. "See baby? I told you that you liked it."

She got off the bed and crawled under me. I was looking down into her cum filled snatch when her lips wrapped around my cock and I almost immediately came. She pulled her mouth off me and coughed:

"Damn baby, that was quick. You must like Darnell plowing your pooper," and she took me back in her mouth and went to work at getting me up again.

I must have really looked a sight. On my knees in a sixty-nine with a woman while her husband was busy trying to cum in my ass while two other black men stood by and watched. Darnell grunted, "Here it comes baby, here comes my love load," and I felt the warm liquid heat fill my butt. Under me Jennifer was screaming and shaking as I ate her, and the two men were standing there with hard cocks standing out in front of them. One of them asked Darnell if they could have a shot at his bitch and Darnell leaned forward and said to me, "They are my friends; help them out please?"

***

By the time it was over, I had come to realize that Jennifer had been right. I liked it, I liked it a lot. The two men were gone and I was lying on the bed swapping tongues with Darnell while Jennifer was alternating between my cock and Darnell's. Darnell broke the kiss and asked:

"Are you my bitch?"

I was silent for a moment and the said, "I guess I am."

"Do you really mean that?"

"Much as it scares me to admit it, I do."

"Then I guess it is time to cement our relationship," and he spun around, pushed Jennifer out of the way and then my cock was in his mouth and he was sucking on it.

I heard Jennifer gasp. "Sweet fucking Jesus. I never thought I would see the day, and with a white man."

Darnell's cock was dangling over my face and I opened my mouth and sucked him in. When he had sucked me dry and I had taken his load, he kissed me and then asked me if I had to leave. I looked at my watch and said that I'd better get going before Martha got worried.

"I don't have any white friends," Darnell said, "or at least I didn't until now. Did Jennifer ever tell you that I only let my friends fuck her?"

"Yes she did."

"She's yours now baby, any time you want, just don't be lying to me about being my bitch."

Just as I was getting ready to leave, Darnell said, "Forget about tomorrow baby and the next time you come by we will have a tape burning party."

"No, I don't think so."

"What do you mean?"

"Tomorrow is still on."

"Are you sure?"

"Yes, I'm sure. Ask Jennifer and she'll tell you all about it. Suddenly, I just have to know."

Chapter 4

The meat was on the grill cooking and the four of us, Martha, Jennifer, Darnell and I, were sitting on the patio working on a pitcher of martinis. Darnell was at his charming best and Martha was enjoying his company. Jennifer sat quietly and watched me to see how I was taking it. I imagined that she was thinking that suddenly I would jump up and holler, "No, I can't do this."

When the pitcher was empty I got up and went in the house to refill it and Darnell followed me in. He moved up behind me and rubbed his cock against my ass:

"Are you sure that you are okay with this? I don't want to risk what we have. If it is going to piss you off, tell me and I'll end it right now."

"No. I really want to know that she won't do it."

"But she will baby; I'm never wrong when I read it in their eyes. It is a done deal baby, but as much as I get a charge out of scoring white pussy, I don't want to lose you over it. Shit! Would you just listen to me? I've got the sexiest, most sexual woman in the world for a wife and here I am infatuated with a fifty year old white man."

"You're confused? I'm married to a woman so sexy that even you want to fuck her, and I'm standing here with you rubbing your cock on my ass, wishing my pants were off so you could fuck me."

Darnell laughed, "We sure are a weird fucked up pair, aren't we?"

"We might have a problem."

"What?"

"What happens if you are right and I am wrong?"

"No problem sweetie. I fuck her during the day while you are at work and then you and I play after you get off."

"Doesn't sound fair to me. You would have her for eight hours and I would only be with you for two."

"You aren't losing, lover. You still get Jennifer at lunch."

It occurred to me that I was already accepting that he was going to fuck Martha. It was a very unsettling thought.

***

After we had eaten and had gone through another pitcher of martinis, I played my part.

"I'm feeling a little woozy. I think I'll go lie down for a while."

Jennifer said, "I guess we should be going anyway."

"Oh no, don't make me the party pooper. You all just sit and enjoy yourselves. If the wooziness goes away I'll come back down."

I went into the house and up to the bedroom. I sat down on the bed, propped myself up against the headboard and started reading a book. From that point, everything went the way Darnell said it would. An hour later I heard someone coming up the stairs and I put down the book and pretended to be sleeping. Martha came into the room and checked on me, kissed me on the forehead and left.

Ten minutes later I heard car doors slam and then the house was real quiet. I got off the bed and went downstairs and found a note propped up on the kitchen table:

"Sweetie, we've gone looking for a place we can get some drinks and music to dance to. See you later. I love you."

The plan (as Darnell outlined it to me) was to find a bar with a band, have a drink or two and then Darnell would go to the men's room, call Jennifer on her cell phone and tell her she had a family emergency. They would leave the bar, drive to Darnell and Jennifer's so that Jennifer could pick up her car. Darnell would invite Martha inside for a drink while Jennifer made a phone call or two, and then Jennifer would leave. If Darnell was right in his reading of my wife, ten minutes after Jennifer goes, Martha would have her legs up on Darnell's shoulders.

An hour and ten minutes later, the phone rang and it was Jennifer: "You want to watch real time or will the tape be okay?"

"What do you mean, 'Watch it real time?'"

"I'm in the room where we have the cameras set up and I'm watching the slut you are married to on her knees and sucking my husband's cock. You want to come over or wait and watch the tape?"

Suddenly I didn't feel good. I was so certain that Martha wouldn't do it, and now she had. "No Jennifer, I'm right in the middle of something I need to finish. I'll wait and watch the tape."

I went up to our bedroom, laid down on the bed and for the first time in thirty-five years I cried.

Martha came home at five-thirty in the morning and I pretended to be asleep. She undressed, got in bed with me, put her arms around me and snuggled up tight to me, and in minutes she was softly snoring.

**

I was up early the next morning and I got out of the house before Martha woke up. I didn't want to be there when she got up because I couldn't bring myself to face her. She had cheated on me! Just how stupid is that? My wife of over thirty years cheats on me and I get upset even though for the past three weeks I've been cheating on her wholesale. It was irrational of me and I knew it, but she was my wife for God's sake. I know, I know, really stupid of me, but Jennifer worked on me for weeks before she maneuvered me into a situation where she could make her play. Martha on the other hand was on her knees with Darnell's cock in her mouth less than two hours after I'd gone up to our bedroom.

That told me things I didn't really want to know or face up to. If Martha was that easy, I could not believe that it was her first time. Up until three weeks ago I had been completely faithful to Martha for over thirty years, but I now doubted that she could say the same. That line of thinking brought up two other questions. If Darnell wasn't her first infidelity, when had her first occurred, who and how long and why had I never had an inkling? And of course there was the million dollar question – what now?

The worst of it was that it was my own fault. I had never doubted Martha, not for one second. I knew she wouldn't, I just knew it. But Jennifer said that Darnell was never wrong when he read a woman. It was a one hundred percent certainty, she said. Darnell indicated that it would be a piece of cake. After everything that the two of them had done to me, regardless of the fact I ended up being a willing participant, I wanted to take them down a peg. So I said go ahead knowing that they would fail, and I could laugh at them and say, "See? I told you." Darnell had even given me one last chance to stop it, but I was still so sure of Martha that I smiled and said go ahead. All I had to do in the kitchen was say, "Better for our relationship if you don't" and it never would have happened. Martha might still have been an unfaithful slut, but I would never have known. And believe me when I say that not knowing was a hell of a lot more comfortable than knowing.

***

There isn't a whole hell of a lot you can do to kill time on a Sunday morning and I had exhausted my options by noon. I couldn't avoid facing Martha forever, so I headed on home. There wouldn't be any confrontation because I was honest enough with myself to know that I had no business throwing the first stone; but even though Martha didn't know it, our relationship had changed and even I didn't know where it was going.

Martha was up when I got home. She greeted me with a kiss and:

"Feeling better, I take it?"

"Some. What time did you get home last night?"

"I don't know. Sometime after the bar closed. Why?"

"I got up to go to the bathroom at ten after four and you weren't home, so I wondered is all," and I went into the den and busied myself with some work I'd brought home.

At five Martha called me for dinner. She had a bottle of wine opened, which is not usual with our meals, and I pointed to it and asked:

"What's the special occasion?"

"You seemed a little out of sorts today. I thought the wine might mellow you out a bit and then I could take advantage of you. I want your body."

"Why on Earth," I said, with emphasis on the right words, "would you want *my body*?"

The implication in my tone was, "Given all you got last night, why would you want me right now?"

I saw her look into my face and in her eyes I read "Could he know?" and then she said, "We always make love on Saturday and we missed last night."

"Yeah, we did, didn't we," I said with emphasis on the 'we'.

Not much else was said during the rest of the meal. After dinner I went back into the den, but I didn't get much work done because I kept seeing Martha's face and the expressions that passed over it during the meal. They said, "He suspects, but he couldn't possibly know, could he?"

It was bedtime before I took myself out of the den. Martha was already in bed when I got there. She had the covers pulled all the way up to her chin and she waited until I was undressed and then she threw them off.

"Ta da!" she exclaimed. She was wearing nylons, a garter belt and her black "Come fuck me" pumps. "You always said that when I dressed like this I would give a stone statue a hard on. Give you any ideas, lover?"

Of course it did. I was upset at what she'd done, but I wasn't stupid enough to let that make me pass up on the best piece of ass I'd ever had. It seemed to be a tad more intense on Martha's part than it usually was, but that could have just been my imagination. That night was the first night in a long time that we did the full range of our sexual experience. She sucked me, I made love to her, and we sixty-nined and I made love to her again. I ate her until I was hard and she asked me to take her ass. When I finished, she got out of bed, got a wash rag, cleaned my cock off and then went down on me until I was hard and then she mounted me.

As she slowly worked herself up and down my shaft, she looked down at me and told me that she had strayed and that she knew that I knew or at least suspected. She did not say those words, but the words she did use told me loud and clear. What she said as she slid up and down my pole was:

"You do know that I love you, don't you?" I grunted and humped up at her and she said, "Don't ever doubt it baby, no matter what, don't ever doubt it."

***

Jennifer was waiting for me in the parking lot Monday morning. She slid into my pickup and leaned over and kissed me. Then she sat back and said:

"Sweetie, can I ask you a big favor?"

"I don't know, what?"

"Don't watch the tape of Martha."

"Why would I want to do you that favor? Given everything that you and Darnell have done to trick me since this all started, why would why would I just take your word for it that Martha was unfaithful?"

"Things between us have changed baby, in ways I can't even begin to understand. Darnell doesn't want you hurt and what Darnell wants, I want. Also, regardless of what you may believe, I do like you. I'm sorry that I caused you pain, but that said, know that I would do it all over again if that is what Darnell wanted. I don't know the depth of your feelings for Martha, but I'm Darnell's, body and soul, because I want to be. If something happened that took him away from me I would die, and that isn't just a figure of speech baby, my feelings for him are that strong. If he told me to go find a pony and give it a blow job I would go out and find a pony. Do you understand what I'm trying to say?"

"No Jennifer, no I don't."

"If you have strong feelings for Martha, be happy with what you have. Don't take a chance on ruining things."

"The tape is that bad?"

"Not to me baby, because Martha and I are two of a kind and I know where she is coming from, but to you? I can only guess baby, but I don't think you will be happy when you see it. I think it will shake you to your core. I've caused you enough pain; I don't want you to suffer anymore. Please don't watch it baby."

"You know what the problem is here, Jennifer? You have burned me too many times so I can't afford to believe you now. Remember the Uncle Remus story about Brer Rabbit and how he begged Brer Fox not to throw him into the briar patch? And how the fox threw him into the briar patch because he thought the rabbit was terrified of the patch? That's where we are here. Are you saying this because you don't really want me to see the tape, or are you doing it to make sure that I want to see it? I don't know the answer to that so I have to see it."

"Okay baby, I tried. Can you take the afternoon off as vacation time?"

"Why?"

"The tape is over five hours long. If you wait until after work it will take you three days to watch it."

***

I followed her into the house and noticed how quiet it was. "Where's Darnell?"

"He isn't here. He won't be home until sometime after six. Hopefully we will be done watching the tape by then." She caught my questioning glance, "I didn't want him here for this."

"Why not? Do you expect me to attack him?"

"No, just the opposite. He can't seem to keep his hands off of you. I'm at a loss to understand it. Until you came along, he had no use at all for whites. Oh he would fuck every white woman he could, but that was mostly for the pleasure he got from taking a white man's woman."

"If he didn't like whites, how did he end up with you?"

"Simple baby, I'm not white, at least as far as the white man is concerned. I have Negro blood in my veins so to the white man that means I'm black. Anyway, back to the subject at hand. You need to watch the tape without any distractions. You don't need Darnell trying to stick his cock down your throat or up your ass, and you definitely don't need him going down on you like he did the last time you were here. I'll put the tape in and sit beside you on the couch unless you want me to leave. I'd like to be here because maybe I can explain a thing or two, but I'll leave if you want me to."

"Explain some things?"

"You'll see baby, you'll see."

***

The tape started with Martha, Jennifer and Darnell coming in their front door and going into the living room. Jennifer went to the phone and faked a call to her sister and after a two minute pretend conversation she hung up. She said she had to go to her sisters and watch her sister's kids while her sister went to the hospital to stay with her mother in law. Darnell turned to Martha:

"Do you mind waiting here until Jennifer gets to her sisters and we see if there is anything else that needs to be done? As soon as she calls I'll run you home."

"No, I can wait a while. Hubby is probably still asleep anyway."

"Okay, I'll call as soon as I get there and see what is happening," Jennifer said as she grabbed her purse and headed for the door.

Darnell got up and went to the front window and looked out. A minute later he turned and said "She's gone" and began to unzip himself. "You want it here or in the bedroom?"

"That's it? That's all the romance I get? No slow seduction?"

"Time is wasting baby."

Martha stood up and pulled her sweater over her head and began unhooking her bra. "Well we certainly don't want to waste any time, do we. Let's start here and work our way to the bedroom."

I sat there stunned at the quickness of it all. From the time Jennifer left until Martha had her legs up on Darnell's shoulders and he had his cock sliding into her cunt, it was less than a minute – less than sixty seconds! I looked over at Jennifer but all she could do was shrug. I turned back to the tape. It was pretty much like the porn videos that Martha and I sometimes rented, only this one was starring my wife.

Darnell fucked her, she sucked him hard and he fucked her again. She took him from behind, she rode him, they went sixty-nine and then Darnell fucked her again. She gave head, she pushed her cunt at him and she took him up her ass. Martha is a noisy fuck, but not a vocal one, if you know what I mean. Lots of grunts, little and loud cries, moans and groans and an occasional "Fuck me hard damn you."

I watched as Martha showed me just how big a slut she could be, but regardless of what they were doing up there on that TV screen, the only thing that really stayed with me was, "Less than a minute – less than sixty seconds!" and what that really meant. It meant that Darnell was by no means the first. It meant that my wife was an easy piece of ass. It meant that all those years I had been a faithful husband, I'd also been a cuckold. No one who could lie down as quickly as Martha had could be a stranger to strange cocks and I wondered how long it had been going on.

On the screen, the action had come to a stop. Martha and Darnell were lying on the bed next to each other. Martha was up on an elbow looking down at Darnell and playing with his limp dick trying to find some life in it. Darnell reached over and rolled her right nipple between his fingers:

"Have you always been this easy?"

"No, usually a guy has to work a little harder to reach the Promised Land."

"Damn. Here I was hoping that I was your first."

Martha laughed, "Honey, the only way you could have been first was to have known me twenty years ago."

"You have been hanging horns on him for twenty years? Does he know?"

"No, and he better never find out either."

"At least tell me I'm your first black man."

"Sorry sugar, that was fifteen years ago."

"Why in the world would you stay with someone for twenty years if he couldn't take care of you in bed?"

"That's a two-parter, honey. First part is that I love him and I don't want to spend my life with anyone else. The second part is that he does just fine in bed. The problem is that he is a mere mortal and not a super being."

"What the hell does that mean?"

"Well, look at you. We've just spent the better part of two hours fucking up a storm. I'm ready to go again and I'm lying here fondling your cock trying to get you up again and you are not responding. My problem honey, is that I need more sex than any one man can give me."

"What you are saying then is that you can fuck for twenty-four hours and he can't? Hell, I can't; no man can."

"That's pretty much it honey."

"And you want more right now and you could go for a couple of more hours?"

"Indeed I could."

Darnell got up and started to leave the room and Martha asked him where he was going. "To get a pep pill and swallow a handful of vitamins. I don't want to disappoint you."

Darnell left the room and was back in about three minutes. He found Martha lying on the bed rubbing her clit. "Whoa, starting without me?"

"Not starting honey, just trying to keep it going."

Darnell got back on the bed and pushed Martha's hand away from her twat and he plunged a couple of fingers into her. She gave a low moan and groaned, "Not a cock, but it does feel good."

"God woman, you are such a slut."

"I know I am honey, but how did you know? How did you know I wouldn't jump up and run for the door when you hit me with that smooth, subtle approach of yours?"

"Your eyes baby, your eyes gave you away."

"My eyes?"

"Yeah. I saw you at the company picnic and I saw your eyes as you checked out every guy there. I knew then I could have you if I could just get you alone. I made up my mind right then and there that I was going to fuck you."

"That picnic was three months ago honey. What took you so long?"

"I had to find a way to meet you and get you alone. My smooth ass approach doesn't work well any place but in my own house."

"Are you telling me that you set today up and arranged my being here?"

"That's it baby."

"How?"

"I had my wife get close to your husband and become friends."

"Just what do you mean by 'get close'?"

"Hey, do I detect a hint of jealousy there?"

"Not jealously, honey. Possessiveness. That is my private stock."

"Isn't that kind of selfish of you? You've been fucking other men for twenty years and you begrudge your hubby a little on the side?"

"I've already explained it honey. If he had any left over when I've had my fill, he could go and spread pollen and I wouldn't care, but I need every bit of him there is. He's mine and you had best keep your little sexpot away from him or I'll scratch her eyes out."

There was a pause, several seconds of silence and then, "Oh shit! If this is a set up then she is in on it. Where is she?"

"Would you believe that I sent her over to keep your husband company?"

Martha quickly sat up. "I'll kill her, I'll kill the bitch," and she jumped off the bed and began picking up her clothes.

Darnell jumped off the bed and put his arms around her and held her. "Easy baby, easy. Calm down, I was just joking with you."

"Where is she? I want to know where she is."

"In the spare bedroom reading."

"I want to see her. I want to know for sure that she isn't at my house."

"You sure? It is liable to kill the mood and I was just about ready for you," and he pointed down at his cock which was twitching and trying to rise.

"Mood, smood, I want to make sure that the little bitch isn't with my husband."

"Okay, okay, put your clothes down, get back on the bed and I'll go get her."

Darnell left the room and came back a few minutes later with Jennifer. "See? I was just joking."

Martha looked at Jennifer, "What did Darnell mean when he said you got "close" with my husband? Did you fuck him?"

"No, I just flirted with him a lot and kind of led him to believe that I might fuck him under the right circumstances. Men his age can get kind of stupid when a girl my age acts like she might be interested."

"What would have been the 'right circumstances'?"

"Darnell telling me to."

Turning to Darnell, Martha said, "You would tell her to fuck my husband?"

"If that was what it might have taken to get you here. It is a moot point now."

"Well, if he ever tells you to fuck my husband, you had best not do it," she said to Jennifer. "He's mine and I'm not sharing him with anybody." She paused and then said, "You're okay with this? Me and Darnell, I mean?"

"Yes."

"Why?"

"He has a thing for white women. Better he does it in front of me than behind my back."

"That's it? You go along with it because you can't stop it?"

"There are other benefits."

"Like what?"

"I get the overflow."

"What does that mean?"

Just then the doorbell rang. Darnell looked at his watch. "Right on time," he said as he got up to go answer it.

Martha looked at Jennifer. "Who the hell comes calling at midnight?"

Jennifer smiled and said, "The overflow."

Martha was opening her mouth to speak when Darnell came back into the room followed by five other black men. Jennifer giggled and said, "That's a total of six cocks Martha, and even if you do three-holers that still leaves three for me. That's the overflow."

Martha looked at Darnell. "Don't you think you should have asked me first?"

"Why? If you need as much sex as you say and you have fucking around on your hubby for twenty years, I'm sure that this won't be your first gangbang."

"Yeah, but a girl still likes to be asked."

"You want me to tell them to leave?"

"No. Now that they are here I shouldn't let them go to waste, should I?"

***

The rest of the tape was the two women fucking the six men in all sorts of combinations and positions. The five guys were done long before the two girls were ready to quit and I began to understand some of what Martha had been saying. After almost six hours of continuous fucking, she still wanted more. Darnell offered to call a few more friends but Martha said no, that she had to get home to me.

The scene switched back to the living room, and as Martha was getting ready to leave, Darnell asked when they could do it again.

"That all depends honey."

"Depends on what?"

"My husband."

"I don't understand?"

"This is the first time I've ever done this at night. Up till now I've always done it during the day when he was at work or when he was out of town. I've always been showered, douched and clean when he came home. If he's awake when I get home and wants to make love, I'll have to find some way to put him off without making him suspicious. I can't let him have me after the six of you have so thoroughly fucked me, but I've never, ever, said no to him before. If I think he might be in the least bit suspicious, I just might have to behave myself for a while. If he's sleeping I'll be okay and Monday would work for me. I'll call you and let you know."

The tape ended as the two of them walked out the door.

"He had her again in your driveway when he got her home. I'm guessing that you didn't wait up for her?"

"No, I pretended to be asleep. What is it that you thought I might need explained?

"Right now you are upset at finding out your wife is a slut, but the one thing that should have been real clear to you is that she loves you. She isn't doing what she's doing because you aren't man enough for her, she's doing it because no six men are enough for her. She keeps her slutty side to herself and keeps on loving you and doing the best she can by you. She's been doing it for twenty years and during that time, she has obviously kept you very happy and content, or you wouldn't have been so rock solid in your belief that she wouldn't go for Darnell's line.

"Don't let what you just saw fuck up your relationship with her. Don't play the double standard game, baby. You are having your fun, let her have hers. Speaking of fun, every time I watch that tape I get horny. You haven't fucked me yet and right now would be a good time to correct that."

"Don't think that I don't want to Jenn, but right now I've got a lot on my mind and I don't think that I'll be very good company. Make me a copy of that tape, would you?"

"I already did baby. Take the one that's in the VCR."

***

As I drove home, my mind had so much going through it that it was a wonder that I didn't get stopped by the cops for not paying attention to my driving. When I got home Martha had dinner waiting. I remembered that it was Monday and that she had told Darnell that Monday would be good for her if I wasn't suspicious when she got home. But yesterday, I did give her reason to think that I was, so did she meet with Darnell or not? I wondered if I could tell.

I grabbed her hand and pulled her to the kitchen table and bent her forward over it. I unzipped and took out my cock, pushed her skirt up to her waist and shoved her thong to the side. She gave a little grunt as I entered her and then she moaned "You aren't supposed to have dessert first" and then she started making all the noises that she does when she is being fucked. Noises that I had just finished listening to at Jennifer's. She was wet, but then she was always wet and I couldn't tell if she had been recently fucked or not. And then the thought occurred to me that I had been getting sloppy seconds for over twenty years, so how could I know?

When I was done, we sat down to dinner and I saw Martha looking at me, and I know that I read her expression right:

"He knows something. I just hope to God it isn't what I think it is."

Chapter 5

Tuesday at lunch Jennifer and I went to the motel, and after the obligatory session of foot worship, I got to fuck her for the first time. It was good as far as a piece of ass went but, quite frankly, my Martha was better; a whole lot better. Now I had one more thought to rattle around in my head. This whole mess I was in started because I wanted a taste of Jennifer's sexy twenty-six year old body. Everything proceeded from that: my sucking Darnell, my taking cocks in my ass and my finding out about Martha.

It was enough to make you cry. All the while I had the best pussy at home, and if I had stayed faithful to my wife, nothing would have happened to me. I would have never found out about Martha and my life could have gone happily on. Now it was a fucking mess – a mess of my own making – and if it wasn't enough that I had to worry about my marriage to Martha and where that was going, I had *me* to worry about. Had I been latently bi all my life and somehow Darnell had seen it, much as he had seen what was in Martha's eyes, or was it something else?

I'd not looked at any other man since Darnell took my oral and anal virginity and wanted to try them on. Yet in my kitchen I had wanted to bend over my kitchen table and take Darnell in my ass, and I had been genuinely disappointed when he wasn't there when I went to view Martha's tape. Darnell said he was infatuated with me. Was that it? Was I really BI or only BI *with him*? Did I have a 'thing' for Darnell? Was I really upset with Martha for fucking around on me or was it because she was fucking my man? And just how fucked up was that – me thinking of Darnell as *my* man!

I was totally fucked up and I didn't know what to do.

***

That evening I stopped at Darnell's and the first thing that Darnell asked me was, "Are we cool?"

"Yes. I told you to go for it if you could. I didn't think you had a prayer, and we both know how wrong I was on that. Did you see her yesterday?"

"Yes, and I just left her today about an hour ago. I have a special treat for you."

"I haven't washed yet. Would you like to taste your wife on another man's cock?"

"You alone?"

"Yesterday. Today I had some help."

"How much help?"

"Three guys, but I was the last one in her."

That led to my sucking off Darnell while Jennifer sucked mine and then I ate Jennifer's pussy while Darnell took my ass. Darnell offered to let me butt fuck him, which almost caused Jennifer to faint, but I declined. I don't know why I declined but I did.

I wrestled with the problem all the way home that night. Martha had dinner waiting, but I wanted to see what she felt like after taking on five cocks, so I told her I was going to have desert first.

"I'm sorry honey, but I've had a pounding headache all day and I'm not up to it."

I just looked at her and I hope that she read the look I was trying to send. I was trying for, "Pounding headache my ass. You've had a pounding, but it was by five men." What I said was, "In that case, forget it."

***

For the next three weeks it was more of the same. I'd go to the motel at lunch with Jennifer, do the foot worship thing, get laid and then go back to work. In the evenings I stopped at Darnell and Jennifer's and the three of us would have sex in all kinds of weird positions. Once I fucked Jenn from behind while Darnell was behind me pumping my ass. Several times Darnell had friends over and I got gangbanged.

Darnell was seeing Martha on the average of three times a week either by himself or with a several friends. On the nights following the days when friends were involved, Martha avoided having sex with me, but on the other nights she would drag me into the bedroom and fuck me till I was exhausted. It was toward the end of the third week, on one of the nights when Martha was avoiding having sex with me, when I said:

"You know that you have refused me sex more times in the last three weeks than you did in the previous twenty years? Something the matter?"

I saw actual fear register on her face just before I turned and walked into the den.

I don't know how much longer things would have gone on that way had I not snapped. I totally lost it one afternoon after my motel jaunt with Jennifer. It had been a memorable day in that for the first time, Jennifer had asked me to butt fuck her. I was driving back to work and Jennifer had her feet in my lap, bare toes playing with my exposed cock and my hands started to shake. They shook so bad that I had to pull over to the side of the road. I have no idea why because I wasn't thinking about any of my messed up personal life at the time, but shake they did and I had to sit on the side of the road for almost five minutes before I got to where I thought I could control the car and head for work.

Jennifer kept asking me what was wrong and all I could tell her was that I didn't have a clue. An hour after getting back to work it happened again, only that time I had been sitting at my desk thinking about the tape with Martha and the six guys. I got up and went to the bathroom and sat in a stall until I got myself under control. Half an hour later it happened again, and again I was thinking about Martha and the gangbang. I sat on the toilet and stared at my hands and suddenly I knew what was wrong. It was rage! Rage that I had suppressed over Martha's infidelities finally breaking out. Forget about my conduct, it had taken Jennifer three weeks to break me down. I could have reconciled Martha having a fling with Darnell, but I could not accept twenty years' worth of lying and cheating, and I could never forget the fact that she had given it up to Darnell in less than a minute.

Once again I got it under control, but an hour before quitting time it happened again and that was when I snapped. I got Darnell on his cell and he sounded winded.

"You with her?"

"Yes."

"Alone?"

"No."

"I want you to round up a dozen or more of your friends for the evening. I want a gangbang, lover, I want so many cocks I'll lose count."

"You sure about this?"

"Dead sure baby, dead sure."

***

The shakes didn't come back and I was able to drive home with no problems. It was as if my decision to finally do something had purged my system. I'd not been getting home before seven-thirty since my affair with Jennifer started, and Martha probably thought she had plenty of time to fuck in the afternoon and still get home in time to have dinner on the table. The surprise on her face was evident when she came into the house and found me already home. Also evident was the freshly fucked look that she had.

"Oh, I didn't expect you so early. Obviously I haven't started dinner yet."

"No problem since we are going out anyway."

"Where?"

"It's a surprise."

"What kind of surprise?"

"Now if I told you that, where would be the surprise?"

"No hints?"

"Only that it is something you crave and seem to want."

"Now you have me very curious."

As we headed out to the car I wondered if Martha realized that I had recognized her 'just fucked' look. She kept pumping me all the way to Jennifer and Darnell's and when we pulled up in front she asked:

"Why are we here?"

"Part of the surprise sweetie."

She looked up at the house and then back at me, "I don't know why, but I have an uneasy feeling. What's going on?"

"All questions will be answered within the next couple of minutes. I'll tell you this. You are going to love it." *Maybe not what is going to follow*, I thought, *but the first part should be right up your alley.*

I rang the doorbell and as we stood waiting, Martha looked nervously over at me. I just smiled at her and waited. Jennifer answered the door and was surprised to see the two of us standing there, but she quickly recovered and asked us in. I ushered Martha (actually, I pushed her in front of me) into the living room where Darnell and seventeen other black men were standing around talking. Darnell looked at me, the question plain on his face, but before he could ask it I said:

"Take Little-Miss-I-Can-Never-Get-Enough and fuck her until she begs you to stop," and then I turned and walked out of the house.

I drove to a bar close to the house and had a few beers while I stared at myself in the mirror behind the bar. I wondered what I was going to do with the rest of my life. About ten I went home and tried to find something to keep myself occupied. At midnight I gave up trying to get anything done and I got back in the car and drove over to Darnell's.

There were twenty-three men there and both Martha and Jennifer were being three holed and the rest of the men were standing around waiting for an open hole. I stood there watching. Darnell came up to me.

"I was surprised. I thought it was going to be for you."

"Oh no lover, a couple or three maybe, but no way I'd ever go that many."

"A couple or three? I get to be first?"

I laughed and said, "Hey lover, whose bitch am I?"

"Same room?"

"Why not."

I don't even know if Martha even saw me getting it at both ends while the guys took her three holes in steady succession. There was a break in the action and I looked over and saw Jennifer looking at me as she sucked the cock of the man standing in front of her. The man said he was going to cum and Jennifer took his cock from her mouth, aimed it at her feet and stroked him until he came. She beckoned me with a finger and said:

"Suck my toes lover, take care of my feet like only you can."

I looked over at the bed where Darnell and two of his buddies were fucking the mindless piece of meat they had turned my wife Martha into, and then I crawled over to Jennifer and started licking her toes.

As I was heading for the door Darnell said, "What about her?"

"Until she begs you to stop or until the last man can't get it up anymore, you can bring her home or send her in a cab."

"Why? Why did you do this to her?"

"That tape has been eating at me like a festering sore since I watched it. The wound needed to be cauterized and this was the way I decided to do it. See you later," and I left.

***

Martha wasn't home when I got up. I showered, dressed and made myself some breakfast and then I called work and told them that I wouldn't be in that day. I was sitting at the kitchen table writing a note to Martha when the front door slammed. I looked up to see Martha staggering into the kitchen.

"You bastard! How could you do that to me?"

I wadded up the note and tossed it aside, and then I picked up the tape from the table and waved it at her. "It was easy Martha, all I had to do was watch *this*. Why don't you watch it and see if you still want to ask the same question again."

I tossed her the tape and left her standing there looking at my back as I left the house. I don't know if she had any questions or not because I never went home.

I hit the post office and rented a box and then filled out a form to have my mail forwarded from the house to the post office box. Next I went to the bank and took out half the cash in the checking and savings accounts, and cashed in four of the seven certificates of deposit that were in the safe deposit box. I swung by work and quit and made arrangements for my final check to be mailed to me.

Jennifer wanted to know what was going on and I told her that I would see her at lunch and tell her all about it. It was bullshit, of course, because when I left the office I headed out of town. I had already loaded the clothes and whatever else I wanted in my truck before Martha had gotten home.

That was four months ago, and I'm living and working in a town seven hundred miles away. I haven't contacted anyone to tell them where I am because I don't want any of them to know. I took out a post office box and made the arrangements to have my mail forwarded from the box in my former town. Martha finally figured out that I was having my mail forwarded and she wrote me a letter and addressed it to the house so it would be forwarded to me. It was full of the type of bullshit that I didn't want to hear:

"I love you, I miss you, I'm worried sick about you. Please call me and at least talk to me. You know I love you and I know we can work things out if you will just talk to me."

There isn't a chance in hell of that happening because even though I do love Martha, miss her terribly and it kills me to wake up in the morning without her beside me, I will never be able to put that "Less than sixty seconds" out of my mind. Nor will I ever forget the ease with which she took on that gangbang. No – an affair I could have worked through, but not what she had been doing for twenty years.

Breaking away from the destructive relationship I was in with Darnell and Jennifer has done me a lot of good too. I'm feeling better about myself and I've had no bisexual urges since getting away from them. In fact the only urges I've had recently are for two of the women I'm now working with. Both seem interested, and the one thing I've noticed about both of them is that neither one has sexy feet when they wear open toed sandals. Thank God for that.

~~The End~~

Here is a sample from another story you may enjoy:

Erotica Short Stories, *Vol. 25*

Just Plain Bob

Stepping Out

My Wife's Erotic Adventures

I don't even remember what it was that triggered my suspicions, but one day I was a happily content husband and the next I was watching everything that Belinda did. I was sure that she was having an affair. I was checking her email on the house computer, looking in her purse when she wasn't around, checking out the glove box and the trunk of her car and even that cliché of cliché's – checking out her clothes in the laundry hamper. I found nothing.

But even after finding absolutely no evidence that she was betraying me, there was something in the back of my mind that told me that Belinda was being untrue. There was an upside to my suspicions; I made love to Belinda more often just to see if I could find her unaccountably wet or loose. The more I made love to her the more she wanted to make love and our sex life did a 180-degree turn and went from twice a week to four and five times a week. As enjoyable as the increased amount of sex was, it did not change the fact that I just knew that Belinda was cheating on me and I wanted proof before I accused her of it.

After two months of trying to find some trace of evidence and not finding any, I was forced to admit that I might just be wrong. I decided to take one last shot at finding out and if nothing happened I would accept the fact that I was a paranoid asshole. I decided to set up an opportunity for her and then be where I could observe.

The simplest way to do it was to set up a phony three-day business trip. That would leave Belinda with plenty of free time on her hands and I would make sure that I was in a position to see what she did with it. The first step was to give her plenty of advance notice so she could make her plans. The day of the trip came and Belinda drove me to the airport, kissed me goodbye and told me to hurry home and she would keep the bed warm for me. As soon as she was out of sight I caught the courtesy bus to a rental car agency and rented a small compact car. Our neighborhood was full of small compacts and one more parked on the street would go unnoticed. From the car rental I drove to a motel and checked myself in for three days and then I headed for home. I hoped to be in place to follow Belinda, but when I got back to the house the car was gone. I parked just up the street and walked back to the house and let myself in and then I went through the house to see if I could find anything that might tell me where she had gone.

In our bedroom, I found that she had laid out several of her sexiest outfits on the bed and I surmised that she had picked out one and was even then wearing it. The question was for whom and where? I was prowling through the hall closet looking in coat pockets for notes or scraps of paper with phone numbers on them, anything that might give me clue when I heard the automatic garage door opener start to operate. I hurried up the stairs and positioned myself where hopefully I wouldn't be noticed and looked down into kitchen/dining room area. I saw Belinda come in with an armful of shopping bags and set them down on the kitchen table and then she went over and picked up the phone and punched in a number.

"Hello darling, I'm home."

"Yes, he got off all right. I dropped him at the airport three hours ago and just before I left to go shopping, I called the airline to make sure that his flight got off on time."

"You do huh? What's in it for me?"

"Promise? All right, but you had better follow through."

"Love you too baby, hurry, I'm already wet just thinking about you."

That was it. I had what I needed.

If you enjoyed this sample then look for **Stepping Out**.

Also by this Author:

The Prodigal Family: The Abbotts

Watching My Shared Wife

The Waitress and the Runaway Husband

Baiting Mr. Little

Too Hot for Henry

Chuck's Fantasy

The Redhead's Desires

Rescued at Riley's

His Every Fantasy

Open Mike Night

Pursuit for Revenge

Why Does He Do That?

Halloween & Drugs

Tracey

When Rob Met Kari

Becoming a Shared Wife, Vol. 1 –

(Wife Sharing and Other Adventures)

Becoming a Shared Wife, Vol. 2 –

(Hazardous Wives)

Becoming a Shared Wife, Vol. 3 –

(Wives Who Stray)

Becoming a Shared Wife, Vol. 4 –

(Fulfilling Her Needs)

Becoming a Shared Wife, Vol. 5 –

(Rachel)

Becoming a Shared Wife, Vol. 6 –

(Sharing My Wife)

Becoming a Shared Wife, Vol. 7 –

(Sarah)

Becoming a Shared Wife, Vol. 8 –

(Cuckolds & Shared Wives)

Becoming a Shared Wife, Vol. 9 –

(Her Forbidden Fantasy)

A Just Plain Bob Christmas

Barbara Jean

Filthy Steps in the Office

My Perfect Wife: And Her Dirty Little Steps

Annabelle Gets Caught

All Filled Up!

Patio with a View

Boyfriend's Corrupted Steps

Never Never

His Wife's Doppelganger

Just A Back-up Guy

Secret Revenge

Becoming a Shared Husband, Vol. 1 –

(Suck Me)

Becoming a Shared Husband, Vol. 2 –

(Husbands Who Stray)

Becoming a Shared Husband, Vol. 3 –

(Get even!)

Becoming a Shared Couple, Vol. 1 –

(Steamy Swingers)

Becoming a Shared Couple, Vol. 2 –

(The Share Thing)

Becoming a Shared Couple, Vol. 3 –

(Kathy is Wild)

Erotica Short Stories, Vol. 1 –

(Taboo Desires)

Erotica Short Stories, Vol. 2 –

(Nasty Steps)

Erotica Short Stories, Vol. 3 –

(Married But...)

Erotica Short Stories, Vol. 4 –

(Sizzling 10)

Erotica Short Stories, Vol. 5 –

(In My Wife's Panties)

Erotica Short Stories, Vol. 6 –

(Taboo Unlimited Desires)

Erotica Short Stories, Vol. 7 –

(XXX Stories)

Dirty Love

Hot & Tight

Her Illicit Adventures

What I Want To Do To Her

Too Fun To Give Up

Creamed

Stepping Out

Yes, I write about sluts and whores because as everyone knows, you tend to write about the things you know. And I do like sluts and whores, just not the ones that lie to me and cheat on me.

So be forewarned - if you click on a Just Plain Bob story you will be getting sluts, whores and husbands who do not kill, maim and destroy. There are other things you will rarely find in a Just Plain Bob story.

If you enjoyed any of my books then please share the love and promote my books in Amazon. I would really appreciate your honest reviews, too!

Good news is always welcome.

One Last Thing, For Kindle Readers...

When you turn the page, Kindle will give you the opportunity to rate this book and share your thoughts on Facebook and Twitter. If you enjoyed my writings, would you please take a few seconds to let your friends know about it? Because... when they enjoy they will be grateful to you and so will I.

Thank you!

Just Plain Bob
justplainbob@awesomeauthors.org

You may also like the books by these authors:

CHOSEN TO BE

Christy's

EXTRA LOVER

HOT SEXY EROTICA

JOAN VEGAS

As I pondered what Ben was asking me about setting up a gang bang for Christy, I knew Andy and Mark would eagerly join in. But how would I discretely recruit other guys? Ben was asking me to line up at least 6 guys, in addition to me and him. I told Ben I would try. He wanted me to set it up about 5 or 6 weeks later, when he knew he would be home. And, he told me to not mention anything to Christy about our plans. He wanted to surprise her.

A few days later, I told Mark and Andy about my mission for Christy. When I told them they would be invited, they whooped and hollered. They both said they could hardly wait. I asked if they had any suggestions on how I could line up four more guys. They both suggested other guys at our school. I wasn't so sure I wanted other guys from our school knowing about the sweet deal I had with Christy and Ben.

Then Mark suggested that we put a discrete ad in one of the local alternative newspapers that was read by younger people throughout the Chicago area. After mulling over the idea, we pooled our money to place this ad for a couple of weeks: "Pretty gal wants more than one guy…soon. Write to P. O. Box ___ for details."

To our happy surprise, one of the newspapers took our ad. A week after the paper came out, the three of us got together to open the replies we had received. Wow…9 of them. Some of them included face and/or dick pictures. I was amazed. We set aside replies from older guys and married guys. We designated four of them as good prospects.

The next week, we received eleven more replies. Most of them had understood that "The pretty gal" was looking for a gang bang. They were all eager to participate. That time, we ruled out seven of them. That left us with a total of eight prospects (not counting Mark, Andy and me). I decided to contact Ben and get his opinion before we met with any of the respondents.

Again Ben and I met for a beer…alone. I told him I had two friends who were enthusiastic about the idea of helping to fulfill

Christy's wish. Then I gave him the eight envelopes we had selected. He agreed that ten guys (plus he and I) might be a bit overwhelming for Christy. He set aside three of the envelopes and said, "How about if you and your friends 'interview' these other five guys." I agreed, and we finished our beers.

That evening, Ben and I had lots of fun with Christy as we winked at each other when she was turned away, knowing what we were planning for her. We made sure she got her share of orgasms that night before we each drained our nuts inside her velvety love channel.

The next day Andy, Mark and I met. I told them about Ben's decisions. We decided on a bar where we could discretely meet with the selected guys…one at a time over the next several days. They each took two guys to call, and I took one. One of Mark's contacts proved to be a flake, so we dropped him.

Over the next week, we met individually with the four remaining guys. They all seemed clean, discrete, and personable. Most importantly, they were all very eager to share in fulfilling "Mindy's" desire to be screwed by several guys. (Yes, we changed Christy's name so no one could ever come back on her.) We got their contact phone numbers, told them the tentative time, and told them we would be calling with a hotel location where we would be meeting.

Ben arranged for a hotel suite and told Christy to be ready for an extra special evening with me and him giving her lots of passionate loving. She bought it.

Shortly after Ben and Christy arrived in the hotel room, I came in (I had my own key card). He and I necked with her while stripping off her clothes. We got her onto the middle of the large bed and Ben began to eat her. I told them I had to go get some ice for our drinks, and left Christy to enjoy Ben's oral ministrations.

I ran downstairs and met Mark and Andy. I brought them to the suite and had them quietly remove their clothes as I made noise mixing drinks for Christy and Ben. In the background, Andy and Mark were both stroking themselves to hardness. I walked into the bedroom with a drink in each hand saying, "You guys ready for some liquid refreshment?" They both sat up and reached for a drink.

Then I looked at Christy and asked, "Are you ready for some extra pleasure?" That was my cue to Mark and Andy. They walked in behind me, totally naked, with boners sticking out in front of them. I said, "Christy...this is Mark and this Andy...my friends...here to give you some extra pleasure." Christy grinned at my nude friends. Ben had already stood up. He said, "Christy baby, I hope you enjoy this special evening," and he sat in a nearby chair.

Andy dove between Christy's outstretched legs and began to lick on her pussy. Although I was still dressed, I got on the bed, cuddled Christy into my arms, and gave her a big kiss. Meanwhile, Mark laid on the bed on the other side of Christy and began caressing her body. He took one of her hands and wrapped it around his stiff dick.

Christy whispered into my ear, "What's going on?" I told her, "Tonight you are going to get your vagina eaten and screwed to your heart's content. Enjoy yourself." She grinned at me before rolling to face Mark. "You are Mark, huh?" she said, while squeezing his dick. "My," she said, "your dick is very hard. I'll bet you know how to use it." She threw her arm over his shoulder and gave him a hot kiss.

If you enjoyed this sample then look for Chosen To Be Christy's Extra Lover.

"Jay! Phone!" I called out to my roommate Jay who was packing for a trip to Florida.

"Who is it?" He yelled back.

"Sara!"

Jay came walking into the room with a worried look on his face.

"No, it can't be this week," he said as he grabbed the phone. "Hello, Sara? Please tell me you - you are at the airport now. Damn, I could have sworn you were coming next week. I have a wedding to go to, I'll be gone all weekend. I know you can't fly back - I'm sure -," he looked at me. "I'm sure Chris won't mind hanging out with you for the week," he quietly said as he walked out of the room.

I'm sure that Sara was not thrilled about spending the weekend with me. It's not like we have issues with each other, we just have not really met before. I have probably said three words to her, all over the phone. Jay came back into the room and put the phone on the table.

"Listen man, I didn't know that Sara was coming this week. I need you to keep her entertained for the next few days. I'm the only person she knows in this state and I don't want her staying alone in a hotel room or something," Jay said as he ran back to the bedroom and grabbed his suitcase. "You can pick her up after you drop me off."

"No problem, I'm sure we could find something to do," I said while standing up and grabbing my car keys. "Let's go."

Jay grabbed me by the arm and stopped me.

"I owe you man. Just be nice to my cousin, she can be a little shy. My aunt and uncle are very strict parents and she isn't great at making friends. She won't really open up unless she trusts you," he told me in a serious tone.

"Don't worry; I'll make her feel at home," I said with a smile.

We left the apartment and headed downstairs to my old Ford Taurus. Jay loaded his suitcase in the back and climbed aboard. We headed off for what should have been a half-hour drive to Los Angeles International Airport. It was noon on a Friday so the traffic heading into the city was a mess, not that it isn't a pain all day every day.

After a delay, we arrived at the airport just shy of 1:00 in the afternoon. His flight was not until 3:00 so he still had plenty of time to get through security. I followed him around the airport until he found Sara. I had never seen her before so I had no idea what to expect. She was a pretty short girl, probably no taller than five-foot three. She was definitely cute, not drop-dead gorgeous but very cute and innocent-looking with long black hair that had two blond streaks running down the front. I could not tell how her body looked since she was wearing baggy black jeans and a loose-fitting black hoodie.

Jay and Sara hugged and talked for a few minutes before walking towards me.

"Chris, this is Sara. Sara, this is Chris," Jay said.

"Hi," she softly said, visibly shy.

I could see that her mouth was fitted with braces.

"Hi Sara," I responded.

"Well guys, I got to head off," said my roommate. "See you guys in a week."

Jay headed towards security and left me alone with his cousin.

"Come on Chris, let's get out of here," Sara said while forcing a smile before following me outside.

For the entire hour long ride home, Sara looked out the window and said nothing. Since Jay had told me that she was extremely shy, I did not try to force anything. I knew that when she wanted to talk, she would talk.

Once we made it out of the city, we finally started making good time. In no time, we were at the apartment. I got out of the car and started towards the door but Sara remained in her seat. I walked over and knocked on the window, causing her to jump. She looked up at me from inside.

"Sorry," she said.

I opened the door for her.

"No need to apologize," I told her as I grabbed her bags from the backseat and led her inside.

If you enjoyed this sample then look for **Teaching Sara Love.**

Hot Erotica
George X. Bush

DESIRED
by the Boys
IN THE CABIN

Mary was fed up with being left behind each month while Riley went up to the cabin with his three friends, Mark, Robert, and John, to fish, drink and just have fun. She was only 23 and she wanted some fun, too. She resented being left behind to fend for herself in this way. She poured herself another drink, her third, and flopped down onto the sofa in frustration as she sipped her drink. *I'll show him*, she thought, sipping her drink, a plan coming into her head. Quickly gulping the rest of her drink down, Mary went to her room and quickly threw a change of clothes and some toiletries into a bag, grabbing her pocketbook and keys as she locked the door behind her and got into the car. If she drove steadily, she could be there in three hours and surprise them.

Mary had to stop a couple of times on the way as she felt herself getting tired, but she finally pulled up to the cabin around four in the morning. As she let herself in, she heard the sounds of snoring coming from different areas of the cabin. She was tired and felt a bit ragged from all she had drunk during the evening, so she quietly tiptoed to the bathroom to take a shower. The water felt so good after the long drive and she stood under it enjoying the sensation.

When she got out of the shower and dried herself, she appraised what she was seeing in the mirror. Her long red hair hung down to the middle of her back. She had that pale skin with light freckles that was common to redheads. Her breasts were very full with large pale nipples on the ends. Mary cupped them in her hands, gently squeezing them as her fingers automatically sought out and found her nipples, squeezing them and pinching them, pulling on them as they screwed themselves into large hard knots. Her hands trailed down her flat stomach to where a small thatch of bright red pubic hair used to grow above her pussy. She had no hair on her pussy, having had it removed by electrolysis so that it was as smooth as a baby's. At the top of her slit, her clit hood peeked through her pussy lips and her clit, fat as a pinkie finger, stuck out from beneath its hood. Her hand trailed down and her fingers trailed up through and between her pussy lips, feeling herself and the wetness that was starting. Her legs were long and straight, as were her feet and toes.

Men had always found her beautiful and at the moment she quite agreed with them.

She was still squeezing her breasts with one hand, her other still between her legs when suddenly the door opened and Robert staggered in, completely naked, his cock dangling in front of him, bigger than anything Mary had ever imagined. As he shut the door, he blinked his eyes, trying to clear the fog of alcohol and sleep so he could make sense of what he was seeing.

"Mary?" he croaked, his voice still sounding a bit drunk.

"Hi, Robert," Mary said, frozen where she stood, her hands not moving.

"What're you doin' here?" he asked, slurring his words. "And how come you're naked?"

"Uh, I thought I'd drive up and surprise Riley and I just took a shower," she replied, letting her hands fall to her sides as she stared at his cock which was beginning to grow even larger…

If you enjoyed this sample then look for **Desired By The Boys.**

Hot Erotica

BLACKMAILED
NANNY
SERVICING THE HELP

JACK RYDER

To some people, I guess that you could say that I was born into a life of privilege; a life of financial privilege that is. Dad had made a killing at the very beginning of the computer boom of the early 90's. I was 6 years old when we moved from the suburbs of Los Angeles to our mansion north east of Seattle. Although we were not as rich as the old money millionaires from out east in the Hamptons, Dad's wealth was just beginning to amass. By the time I was ten, he was a billionaire several times over.

Even though our wealth was what you would call "new money", Mom and Dad quickly settled into the lifestyle of the rich and famous. This meant that we now had maids and butlers to take care of the mansion. We had limos with chauffeurs to take us everywhere and anywhere we wanted at any time we wanted. My baby sister Phoebe and I even had a nanny.

Gracie was only 18 when Dad hired her to be our surrogate mother, so to speak. That was really what she was for us since Mom got so busy with her civic duties and private clubs. From the moment that Dad struck it rich; it was like our parents never again had more than a few minutes alone with us. The both of them did try to compensate for this by throwing money and gifts at Phoebe and me but Gracie who ended up becoming our only adult supervision.

At the time, I could never figure out why Gracie stayed with us all these years. From the start, Phoebe was a high maintenance child with an assortment of physical maladies and mental health issues and although I was much better equipped to take care of my own needs, I was an absolute hellion when I was a young preteen.

I constantly found little pranks to pull on Gracie. Rearranging furniture in rooms after she had set things right, adding extra soap to the laundry so it would bubble over. Rearranging things on my father's study desk after she had placed everything exactly the way he wanted them. I could only imagine what hell I put her through back then. After I reached puberty, it got even worse for her. I began peeping on her in the shower and in her bedroom when she was getting dressed.

However, by the time I reached high school, it was a little better for her. Phoebe's psychologist had finally found a combination of medications that made Phoebe much more manageable and I had let up on the pranks. Now, my main interest was finding ways to see Gracie in the nude and taking secret photos of her with either my cell phone or the fancy professional type camera that Mom had given me as a birthday gift.

I guess that you could say that I sort of had a crush on my nanny at this point. Although she was twelve years older than me, she was the prettiest woman I had ever seen. Even though I had plenty of girls at school who were willing to throw themselves at me because my father's wealth, Gracie was the only woman I ever fantasized about. She was the only girl that interested me.

With the way I treated her when I was a kid; I could not understand why she didn't simply quit. Dealing with my family was hard enough for me; I could only imagine what it was for her. I was even more shocked that Gracie stayed with us for so long after I saw exactly what my father was demanding of her. It was just after my 18th birthday and about three weeks before I was going to graduate from high school. I came home from school much earlier than usual that day and Dad happened to be home from one of his many month-long business trips.

I heard soft voices coming from the study as I came up the stairs to my room. "Yes baby...you know what I want."

If you enjoyed this sample then look for **Blackmailed Nanny.**

ANGUS MacGREGOR

RESCUED

HOT ROMANCE EROTICA

THE PARDONED SERIES, BOOK 2

She giggled to herself remembering when she was younger, just really beginning to be curious about boys. One night when Jack had been complaining of allergies, she had intentionally given him way too much Benadryl which knocked him out. She waited until the house was dark and still, and sneaked into his room, pulled back the covers, and cautiously slid his underwear down. She stared at his penis, now large and man-sized, framed with soft brown curls, as it hardened in the cool air and soon lay back against his soft belly. She had no sexual attraction to Jack, but part of her wanted to hold his dick and just see what it felt like. She had the distinct feeling that he wouldn't have minded. She finally stretched out her hand and held the heavy shaft and marveled at how soft and hard it was at the same time stroking the shaft up and down until he was rock hard and a clear drop of pre-cum oozed from the tip. She had thrown the covers back over him and ran to her room, embarrassed and aroused at the same time. As she lie in the quiet of her own bed, she slid her hand down between her legs and rubbed her clit as images of Jack were replaced with Charlie Morris, a handsome boy from her Algebra II class. He sat beside her, and Cassie had noticed that he was constantly adjusting his dick in class. Often when he was asked to go to the whiteboard to work a problem, his erection pressed hard against his jeans revealing a thick round head. She imaged her hand sliding up and down his hard cock, lowering her head to his lap, feeling the heat of his member in her hand and against her face as she brought herself to a shattering climax.

Cassie grinned thinking how much Jack would love that story and would give her hell for being such a perv. He would offer to show her the real thing again any time she wanted, she figured. Her little sister Carly was sweet but interestingly, Cassie didn't feel nearly as close to her. The two of them had hardly ever spoken about boys and sex, whereas she and Jack were always bouncing their exploits off each other. Of course in her case, they were so few she didn't bother saying too much. Jack, on the other hand, enjoyed being as shockingly graphic with her as he could be, but a big part of her enjoyed the playful, dirty talk.

Cassie had a few close calls in high school. The most intense was with Charlie Morris, who had asked her to prom when she was a junior. The two had spent a few fun hours on her bed or his when their families weren't around. The week before prom, he had pulled his dick out, and she finally got to really touch it. He pushed his jeans and shorts down to his ankles and pulled his shirt up to his neck. She knew he wanted her to suck it, but she wasn't sure about that. As she stroked his penis, he softly stroked the lips of her vagina and teased with the opening, which was wet and wanting. She gasped as his finger slid gently inside her as they kissed. Her hand sped up stroking his cock until he groaned. She watched as thick pearly ropes of semen blasted on his firm belly and got caught in the soft light brown hairs that ran from his navel to his groin.

After prom, the two had driven to a logging landing out on Baber Mountain. The night had been warm for May. Cassie had smiled when she saw the planning Charlie had done to for the night. He made a comfy place on the back of his pickup bed. The two sipped some lemon-flavored vodka, which was horrible, and lay with their formal clothes while they kissed and groped each other.

Cassie remembered his penis straining against the thin fabric of the tuxedo pants…

If you enjoyed this sample then look for **Rescued**.

WANT FREE COPIES OF MY BOOKS?
Just visit my blog and download free copies of my books:
awesomeauthors.org/justplainbob